1012545

J822.914   4-8
Aike   Aiken, Joan.
            The mooncusser's
          daughter **DATE DUE**

5.95			
NO 16 '74			
MY 25 '77			
JUN 9 1981			

THE MOONCUSSER'S DAUGHTER

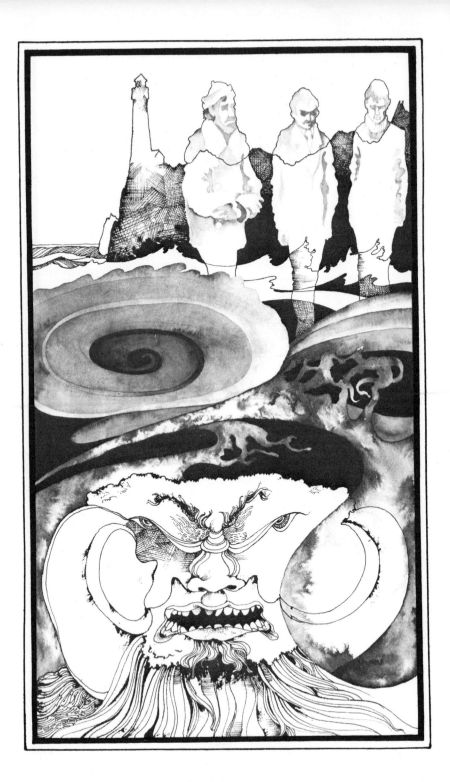

THE MOONCUSSER'S DAUGHTER

A PLAY FOR CHILDREN BY
JOAN AIKEN

ILLUSTRATED BY ARVIS STEWART
MUSIC BY JOHN SEBASTIAN BROWN

THE VIKING PRESS   NEW YORK

FIRST AMERICAN EDITION

TEXT COPYRIGHT © 1973 BY JOAN AIKEN
MUSIC COPYRIGHT © 1973 BY JOHN SEBASTIAN BROWN

First published in 1974 by The Viking Press, Inc.
625 Madison Avenue, New York, N. Y. 10022
1 2 3 4 5 77 76 75 74
Printed in U.S.A.

LIBRARY OF CONGRESS CATALOGING IN PUBLICATION DATA

Aiken, Joan, 1924– The mooncusser's daughter.
SUMMARY: The mooncusser's daughter thwarts the criminals who seek
the treasure hidden in a wreck under her father's lighthouse.
[1. Plays]   I. Stewart, Arvis L., illus.
II. Brown, John Sebastian.   III. Title.
PN6120.A5A33 1973   822'.9'14   73–5146
ISBN 0–670–48795–3

FOR GEORGE NICHOLSON

ALSO BY JOAN AIKEN

BOOKS FOR YOUNG READERS

THE MOONCUSSER'S DAUGHTER

CHARACTERS

SAUL BILKANCHOR, lighthouse-keeper of Sabertooth Light
RUTH, his wife
FRED, Saul's brother, a ghost
SYMPATHY, Saul's daughter, aged about nineteen
LORD BOSS, a king of crime
FEVER ⎫
GRITTY ⎬ employees of Lord Boss
SUNUP ⎭
MACAWMACK, a bird
CALIBAN
WAITER

SETTING: The Seacoast of Bohemia

PRELUDE

ACT ONE

Note: *Mooncusser* was a word used on the New England coast for wrecker.

PRELUDE

Sabertooth Lighthouse is first seen far off, illuminated; then silhouetted. Then complete dark. Ray of light as from revolving lighthouse lantern travels over stage and audience. Darkness.

MAN'S VOICE [*singing*].
> Then three times around went our gallant ship,
> Then three times around went she;
> Then three times around went our gallant ship,
> And she sank to the bottom of the sea, the sea, the sea,
> And she sank to the bottom of the sea. . . .
> Then three times. . . .

WOMAN'S VOICE [*speaking slowly*]. Three times, thrice, one, two, three; three repetitions, first time, second time, third time—

MAN'S VOICE. Then three times around. . . .

WOMAN'S VOICE. Around, around about, around in a circle, around in a ring, around and around, circumscribe, describe a circle, around—

MAN'S VOICE. Then three times around went our gallant. . . .

WOMAN'S VOICE. Gallant, handsome, fine, brave, valiant, heart of oak. . . .

9

MAN'S VOICE. Ship. . . .

WOMAN'S VOICE. Boat, vessel, bark, brig, schooner, liner, submarine—

MAN'S VOICE. For heaven's sake—we're thirty seconds over time as it is.

WOMAN'S VOICE. Cut out the last verse then—

MAN'S VOICE. Then three times around went she. . . .

WOMAN'S VOICE. She, her, feminine pronoun, because a ship is always taken to be female.

MAN'S VOICE. Then three times around went our gallant ship
And she sank to the bottom. . . .

WOMAN'S VOICE. The bottom, the lowest part, base, nethermost, final cause, origin, get to the bottom, probe to the root, bottom of one's heart. . . .

MAN'S VOICE. And she sank to the bottom of the sea. . . .

WOMAN'S VOICE. The sea, the ocean, the main, the deep, waves, tides, salt water.

MAN'S VOICE. And she sank to the bottom of the sea, the sea, the sea,
And she sank to the bottom of the sea.

WOMAN'S VOICE. That ends our program of English by radio for seafarers. We'll be back tomorrow at the same time. Now, because we left out the last verse, you'll have to wait two minutes for the next item—news and weather. Good-bye till tomorrow.

[*Silence*]

DIFFERENT MAN'S VOICE. Hello, hello, hello. Caliban, are you there, Caliban? Calling Caliban. Can you

10

answer me, Caliban? Calling Caliban, calling
Caliban. Over.

CALIBAN'S VOICE. Help, help, help. This is Caliban! This
is Caliban. Can you hear me? Who are you?

DIFFERENT MAN'S VOICE. Where are you, Caliban? Where
are you? Can you give me your position? We
want to help you; we're trying to help you.

CALIBAN'S VOICE. I'm in a box, in a ship, in a bottle; it's
deep and dark and very cold. I'm shut in a
box—it's dark; it's dark.

DIFFERENT MAN'S VOICE. Yes, but where is this box,
Caliban? Where it it? Quick, we haven't
much time. Can you give me your position?
Where are you, Caliban? Over.

CALIBAN'S VOICE. Below the cliff, under the whirlpool. Let
me out. Help me, help me, help me.

DIFFERENT MAN'S VOICE. What cliff, what cliff? Can you
tell me, Caliban? We want to help; we want
to get you out.

CALIBAN'S VOICE. Sabertooth Light—the cliff by Sabertooth
Light.

DIFFERENT MAN'S VOICE. What coast? What coast, Caliban?

CALIBAN'S VOICE. Bohemia. The seacoast of Bohemia.

DIFFERENT MAN'S VOICE. How deep do you lie?

CALIBAN'S VOICE [*fading*]. Full fathom five. . . .

DIFFERENT MAN'S VOICE. Hold on, Caliban. We'll be coming
down for you—can't say when but it will be
very soon—just you hold on—wait for
us. . . .

[MAN'S *voice fades, and Big Ben strikes.*]

11

ACT ONE

SCENE ONE

Light increases on one side of stage to show interior of Sabertooth Lighthouse ground floor. Section of curved wall, door at side, window, pair of elevator doors at rear. Stairs to upper gallery with door and suggestions of more stairs going on up. Rocking chair, armchair, small table, cooking stove, gunrack, cradle. Cobwebs everywhere. Sound of sea, gulls, throughout. RUTH BILKANCHOR, *who is blind and wears dark glasses, sits knitting and rocking in rocking chair. She is thin, gentle, in her fifties, white hair plainly arranged, perhaps in a bun.* FRED'S *ghost, dressed as a sailor but all in white, and with a white face, is sitting on the windowsill. He has a white Yo-Yo with which he plays a lot of the time.*

Elevator music [a special tune that is played each time the elevator is in motion] is heard; elevator doors open to admit SAUL BILKANCHOR, *who carries a large bucket.* SAUL *is about the same age as* RUTH, *with long white hair, whiskers, and beard. Doors shut again.*

SAUL [*dumping down bucket*]. He's restless. Off his feed.

RUTH.   Why is that?

SAUL.   Maybe because the whirlpool is moving off a bit, down channel. He thinks he might get away—make a break for it. But he's wrong.

RUTH.   Saul—why don't you let him go? I'm sure it

can't be right to keep him shut up down
there.

SAUL [*violently*]. Are you mad? Let him go? Never!

RUTH. It must be so boring for him down there in
that bottle.

SAUL. No one's going to profit from my crime. Not
me—not *anybody*.

RUTH. But. . . .

SAUL [*pacing about*]. I'm accursed! I'm the outcast of man-
kind. [*He has taken off seaboots and is in
socks with large holes; every now and then
he trips.*] I'm a haunted man, I tell you.

RUTH [*knitting away*]. Yes, you do tell me—often.

SAUL. I'm damned. I'm doomed.

RUTH. Yes, dear.

SAUL. For twenty years a curse has lain on me.

RUTH. Nineteen this March.

SAUL. I'm a reject; I'm a throw-out; I live in exile.

RUTH. That's right.

SAUL. Oh, why did I follow the dreadful trade? Why
did I do it?

RUTH. Well, dear, for ten years you used to say you
did it for kicks. Then, for the last nine,
you've been saying you did it because society
owed you more than a lighthouse-keeper's
salary of four pounds a year with free fishing
and electricity.

SAUL. Free electricity! Pah! I live in a darkness of
my own making, haunted by the thought of
a brother's unforgiving ghost.

RUTH [*patiently*]. Look, Saul, for the umpteenth time, Fred *has* forgiven you. He forgave you right after it happened, nineteen years ago. Didn't you, Fred?

FRED [*moving forward*]. That's right. Never one to bear a grudge, I wasn't. Anyhow—easy berth being a ghost. No worries. Go wherever you like. Except I mostly like to stay here. Better than all that running I used to have to do—bun-running, gum-running, rum-running, gun-running, mum-running—*I'm* certainly not complaining. No more running for old Fred.

RUTH. See? He's forgiven you. He says so.

SAUL [*who can't see or hear* FRED]. Haunted, haunted, I tell you, by my past crimes—[*tripped by his flapping sock, he falls heavily*]. Oh, flaming Hades! Ruth! I wish you'd mend my socks.

RUTH [*calmly*]. Dear, I've told you over and over that mending socks is a thing you just can't do when you're blind. I'm knitting you this new pair, they'll be finished by tomorrow. . . .

SAUL [*taking no notice*]. But still, it's *right* that I should suffer. It's *right* that I should be wretched.

RUTH. Now if you'd allow little Sympathy to come home, I daresay *she'd* do a bit of mending for you.

SAUL. Never!

RUTH. Helpful little thing she used to be.

SAUL. My daughter must never return to this accursed spot.

RUTH [*sighing*]. Fancy not wishing for your own daughter.

SAUL. The dead ground where a crime was committed is no place to bring up a child. Besides, I never did care for brats: always asking questions, wanting piggybacks—or ice cream—losing their balls over the cliff—

RUTH. Anyway, Sympathy's turned nineteen; you could hardly call her a child now. Suppose she's homesick?

SAUL [*pacing about so energetically that* FRED *has a difficult job keeping out of his way*]. I tell you she shall not reenter these tainted walls.

RUTH. Fred, do come and sit by the fire. It makes me nervous when Saul gets like this. I keep thinking he'll tread on you. And you might give little Jennet a bit of a rock; she's wakeful, the angel.

[FRED's *ghost obediently squats and rocks cradle.*]

SAUL. Isn't it nearly dinnertime? I'm devilish hungry.

RUTH. I'll just finish turning this heel; then I'll put on the milk.

SAUL. Bread and milk *again?* Can't we have a change from everlasting bread and milk?

RUTH [*apologetically*]. They're the only things that get delivered. Now I can't go shopping bread and milk's all I can manage—

SAUL [*sourly*]. In that case don't trouble. I'll finish what Caliban left. [*He eats out of bucket with spoon.*]

[*Door opens; a voice shouts* Postman! *and a letter is tossed through.*]

RUTH [*joyfully*]. Oh, it'll be a letter from Sympathy!

SAUL.   How do you know?

RUTH.   Nobody else writes to us. Do read it aloud.
             There's a love.

SAUL.   Why should I? She doesn't write to *me*.

RUTH [*patiently*]. Look, dear, you keep forgetting that for
             the last five years I've been blind. I'd ask
             Fred, but we've tried before; he can't. Go
             on—do—you know you'll like to hear her
             news. I wonder if she's passed her exams.

SAUL [*exasperated*]. Oh—my life is just one long penance.
             But that's right. That's as it should be. [*Picks
             up letter, rips it open.*] "Dear Mum. I hope
             you are well. Why do you never write to me
             anymore?"

RUTH [*sighing*]. Eh, dear—What else does she say?

SAUL [*reading*]. "I have finished at ballet school and got
             my diploma, and I'm fed up with being away
             from home, so I'm coming back for a bit and
             shall arrive on Tuesday. . . ."

RUTH.   Tuesday! But that's *today!* Oh, I am pleased!

SAUL [*still reading*]. "Tell Dad"—*Well,* of all the unnatural,
             spiteful little—I was quite right to send her
             away—

RUTH.   Why? What does she say?

SAUL.   "Tell Dad if he doesn't want to see me he
             can sit up in the lamp room or go down in
             the cave or jump off the cliff, I don't care
             which. Lots of love, dearest Mum, from Sym-
             pathy." Well, that settles it. She's not coming
             here. If I see her coming it's her own respon-

18

sibility—I shall warn her off just as I would anybody else. [*He takes gun—a large bell-mouthed blunderbuss—from rack and goes upstairs.*]

RUTH.   Oh, dear. Has he taken the gun, Fred?

FRED.   Yes.

RUTH.   That's going to be awkward. What shall we do?

FRED.   I dunno.

SCENE TWO

Light shifts to other side of stage. Hotel balcony on edge of cliff. Signs of luxury: plants in gold pots, champagne in bucket. LORD BOSS, *dressed in tropical beachwear, is sitting in elaborate deck chair, shooting sucker darts at a large target. He is a very poor shot.*

LORD BOSS.   Waiter!
             [*Waiter rushes in.*]

WAITER.   My lord?

BOSS.   What have you got on the lunch menu?

WAITER.   Everything—everything, my lord.

BOSS.   I don't believe you. What haven't you got?

WAITER.   My lord?

BOSS.   Come on, come on—Have you got shark's fin?

WAITER.   Yes, my lord.

BOSS.   Long pig?

WAITER.   F-f-fairly long.

BOSS.   Lark's tongues?

WAITER [*doubtfully*]. There's lark *pie;* I daresay we could take the tongues out and serve them separately—

BOSS.   Bird's nest soup? [WAITER *is silent.*] Well, speak up, man. Have you got it or haven't you?

WAITER [*desperately*]. We could have some flown over from China—I'm afraid lunch might be a little late—

BOSS [*dangerously*]. Well, just you *get* some flown over. And lunch had better *not* be late, or it's unlikely I shall stay at this hotel again—it's unlikely *anyone* will ever stay at this hotel again—

WAITER.   Y-y-yes, my lord. . . . [*He starts out, running, then runs back to say*] Three gentlemen you wanted are here to see you, my lord—Mr. Fever, Mr. Gritty, and Mr. Sunup—

BOSS.   About time, too. Well, don't stand there looking like last year's calendar. Send them in. And get that bird's nest by one o'clock—

[WAITER *shows in* FEVER, GRITTY, *and* SUNUP, *then dashes off.* FEVER *is a tough-looking, middle-aged gangster—very short haircut, stubble on chin.* GRITTY *is the youngest of the three; about twenty, with long curly hair and glasses, he has an absentminded expression and may carry a guitar.*]

BOSS.   Well? Did you find out where the book is? Fever?

FEVER.   Yes, boss. [SUNUP *nudges him.*] Er—yes, my lord.

BOSS.   Where is it?

FEVER.   It's like you thought. It's still in the wreck of the *Miranda,* which is lodged in the cave at the foot of Sabertooth Cliff.

BOSS.   Right. Send along a dredger this afternoon and haul the whole wreck up to the top.

FEVER.   Can't do that, my lord.

BOSS [*not pleased*]. Oh? Why not?

FEVER.   There's a whirlpool every high tide. Caliban's Caldron, the locals call it. Any ship gets close to those cliffs is a write-off. The dredger wouldn't stand a chance. They say even the sea serpent got himself corkscrewed down into the whirlpool once and he's never been able to unwind himself since.

BOSS.   Send down a diver then.

FEVER.   He'd get smashed up, too.

BOSS.   For the love of Mercury—Do I have to go *myself?*

FEVER [*hastily*]. No, no, boss. Listen, it's like this. Well, see, the only way to get to the foot of the cliff is from the lighthouse—there's twenty miles of those cliffs, all as sheer as an office block. And the cave's right under the lighthouse— there's supposed to be a way down, a stair or a path or summat—

GRITTY.   An elevator, *I* heard—

BOSS.   And so?

FEVER.   Well, there's some crazy old character in the lighthouse who won't let anyone in. Says there's a curse on the place. Has a blunderbuss. Threatens to shoot anyone who sets foot.

BOSS.   Well, shoot *him.*

FEVER.   That won't wash either, my lord.

BOSS.   Why? *why?*

FEVER.   They say down in this cave there's a big rock, like, balanced on a kind of a spur. Right up above the ship. If this old guy was to do something, pull some lever—

GRITTY.   Let off a firecracker, *I* heard—

FEVER.   The rock falls and the ship's smashed to blazes.

BOSS.   In which case *you'd* be smashed, too. Of that you can be *quite* sure. Well, you'll just have to use cunning. Pretend you're the window cleaner. Get into that lighthouse. Then—

FEVER.   Then that's not the only complication.

BOSS.   A lot of *geniuses* I have working for me. All I want is to get hold of an old book out of a ship that's been lying under water for twenty years—anyone would think I was trying to get the gold out of Fort Knox. Well?

FEVER.   The book has a guardian.

BOSS.   A guardian? You mean there's someone down there in the wreck keeping an eye on it—I

	suppose you're going to tell me it's the sea serpent?
FEVER.	Something of the kind, my lord.
GRITTY.	We managed to get in touch with it on V.H.F. It has a name—Caliban.
FEVER.	Told us it had been left in charge of the book. By the previous owner.
BOSS.	Oh, this is just great. Loonies in the lighthouse, werewolves in the wreck—going to tell me you're scared?
FEVER.	No, but all these difficulties have put the price up. Five thousand we want now.
BOSS.	Three. Not a penny more.

[*The three glance at one another, shake heads.*]

FEVER.	Four. And that's our last word.
BOSS.	You get four, I get the book by this time tomorrow. Otherwise I get me some other helpers. Okay? [*They nod.*] So, where were we?
GRITTY.	We were telling you about Caliban.
BOSS.	*What* about Caliban?
GRITTY.	Caliban says he won't give up the book unless we fetch down somebody that's single in spirit.
BOSS.	Single in *spirit?*
GRITTY.	Those are the rules, he says. Someone free from the taint of deceit.
FEVER.	In other words, some bloke what's never told a lie in all his life.
BOSS.	Then you'll have to find someone, won't you?

FEVER.   Have a heart, guvnor. How are we going to set about that?

BOSS.   There's no reason why I should do your job for you, but as it happens I've got something that might help. [*He goes through balcony door.*]

GRITTY [*begins to wander about, singing to himself*].
    Who is Caliban, who is he?
    Everyone seems to wonder;
    Sleeping down below the sea,
    Snoring away like thunder
    Fifty-five fathoms under—

FEVER.   What beats me is *why* the boss should want an old book that's been down at the bottom of the sea for nearly twenty years.

GRITTY [*singing*].
    Eels he has where he oughta have hair;
    Hands and feet are suckers;
    Breathes in brine instead of air,
    Makes a horrible ruckus,
    Sounds like a boiler in bad repair—
    —I daresay the boss wants that book because it's just about the only thing that he hasn't got already.

FEVER.   Yes, but what does he want it *for*?

BOSS [*reappearing so suddenly that he makes them jump*].
    That book's been at the bottom of the sea a lot longer than twenty years, Fever.

FEVER [*recovering*]. But, like I said, what d'you want it for, guvnor? You're the richest man in the world as it is.

BOSS.   So there's no point in making myself richer, is there? I can't look at a different movie with each eye. Can't sail two yachts at once. Can't drink six glasses of champagne at the same time. [*He is holding a glass paperweight-type ball with a ship inside it, which he tosses to* FEVER.] Hold that, and count ten.

FEVER. One, two, three. . .

BOSS [*simultaneously with* FEVER]. What would you do if you were the richest man in the world, Gritty?

GRITTY. Sit in the sun all day and make up tunes.

FEVER [*dropping the ball, which bounces*]. Stap me, the flaming thing's red hot! Why didn't you say?

BOSS [*retrieving ball, tossing it to* GRITTY]. Hold it and count ten—

FEVER [*rubbing his burnt hand*]. If *I* was the richest bloke in the world, I'd make a big bomb and blow up my old woman.

GRITTY. Four, five, six— you're not burning *my* fingers off. . . . [*He drops the ball in the ice bucket*]. How does it get that way?

BOSS.   I've done everything I can with money. Now what I want is power—

GRITTY. To do what?

BOSS.   Change the weather. Fill in the Mediterranean. Make a ski resort in the Sahara. [*There is a large globe on the balcony; he inverts it, spins it, and sits on top*]. I want to turn the world upside down. Flatten the Himalayas. Melt the ice caps. Chop down all the

forests. See? Now you take that ball and find
me somebody who's never told a lie.

FEVER [*puzzled*]. I don't quite get you, boss.

BOSS.　　　　　Find me somebody who can hold that ball
while they count ten—

SCENE THREE

*The lamp room of the lighthouse. The one huge light, sur-
rounded by a glass chimney like an old-fashioned oil lamp,
is switched off.* SAUL *is polishing the chimney and looking
from time to time out of the window, where he has his
blunderbuss propped.* FRED's *ghost glides in and begins
hypnotizing* SAUL *by means of arm-waving dance.* SAUL
doesn't see it but is insensibly influenced.

FRED [*singing*].
　　　　　Full fathom five thy brother lies;
　　　　　His buttons turned to haddocks' eyes;
　　　　　Nothing of him now is found
　　　　　Save a ghost that floats around
　　　　　Two feet off the ground.
　　　　　Some might find this rather strange,
　　　　　But not old Fred; he likes the change.

[SAUL *slowly falls asleep, leaning farther and farther over
the gun which finally goes off without waking him.*]

SCENE FOUR

Edge of cliff, indicated by one or two tufts of grass and distant view of lighthouse as in Prelude. SYMPATHY *comes in carrying duffel bag, followed by* GRITTY.

SYMPATHY. Well, thanks for the lift. Hope I didn't bring you out of your way.

GRITTY. No, you haven't. As a matter of fact—I want to ask a favor of *you* now—

SYMPATHY. Sure. What is it?

GRITTY. You live in the lighthouse—

SYMPATHY. Well—I used to. But my dad said an awful crime had been committed there and it wasn't a proper place for a child. So he sent me off to boarding school.

GRITTY. I've heard the locals say the lighthouse is haunted—

SYMPATHY. That's right. By my Uncle Fred and my little cousin Jennet. Oh, I *am* looking forward to seeing Jenny again. She was such a little duck—always laughing, never grizzled—

GRITTY. You've *seen* them? The ghosts?

SYMPATHY. Of course. I used to play with Jenny all the time when I was little—

GRITTY. Strewth. Excuse me, would you mind holding

	this a moment while I polish my glasses. [*He pulls glass ball wrapped in a handkerchief from his pocket, unwraps and hands it to* SYMPATHY, *polishes his glasses.*] But why do the ghosts of your uncle and cousin haunt the place?
SYMPATHY.	Uncle Fred's ship got wrecked in the channel. Little Jenny was on board. They were both drowned. I suppose the lighthouse was the nearest bit of land for them to haunt on—
GRITTY.	I see.
SYMPATHY.	But what was the favor you wanted to ask? Not just for me to hold this? [*playing toss and catch with ball*] It's pretty. [*She examines it.*] Uncle Fred's ship is sunk in the big cave at the foot of the cliff. They say a great crystal stalactite has formed all round it, so it's like a ship in a bottle—
GRITTY.	Well I was wondering if you could help me. It's this way—I'm a student of Marine Psychology—doing a research project on dolphins' dreams—
SYMPATHY.	Do dolphins have dreams?
GRITTY.	Why not? You see ghosts. Dolphins have dreams. Thanks—[*He puts on glasses, holds out hand for ball; she tosses it to him; he feels it in amazement, hurriedly wraps it in his handkerchief again, and replaces it in his pocket.*] There's a dolphin out in that chan-

nel, you see. I've got into communication
with it on V.H.F.; now I want to study it face
to face—

SYMPATHY. It's not going to be easy. There's a whirlpool
in the channel—if you aren't careful, you'll
be drowned for sure—

GRITTY. I know. That's why I wanted to get into your
dad's lighthouse—I heard there was a way
down to the cave, thought I might get a look
at the dolphin from there.

SYMPATHY. Yes, Dad built an elevator down so he could
go and look at the wreck and feel miserable—

GRITTY. I went up there, but he fired his gun at me
through the window. So I wondered if I could
come along with you. Maybe you could say
I was a friend of yours. . . ?

SYMPATHY. But you aren't a friend of mine. We've only
just met.

GRITTY [*taken aback*]. Well—but—we might *get* to be
friends. I—I'd *like* to—I could pay you quite
a bit, too. I've got this grant—

SYMPATHY. I'm afraid it wouldn't be possible, I don't
even know if my father will let *me* in. And
he'd *never* stand for my bringing in a boy-
friend—

GRITTY [*swallowing*]. Maybe I could dress up as a girl? Say
I was a school friend of yours?

SYMPATHY. But that would be telling a lie.

[*Deadlock*. GRITTY *looks at her blankly. She smiles good-
bye and goes.* FEVER *and* SUNUP *rise up from behind grass*

*tussocks where they have been concealed. They all look
at each other and shrug.*]
GRITTY [*singing*].

>Let's leave Caliban, let him lie;
>It's tough enough to be him.
>No use dragging him high and dry,
>Nobody wants to see him.
>Bye-bye, Caliban, bye-bye-bye. . . .

FEVER [*uneasily*]. What d'you reckon Caliban *is?*
GRITTY. Some kind of monster? Maybe he is the sea serpent.
FEVER. Why should he want someone who's never told a lie?
GRITTY. To eat? Maybe they're tenderer that way. Crazy bit of luck—that girl's one of these no-lie marathon types—
FEVER [*sourly*]. Except that she wouldn't cooperate.
GRITTY [*airily*]. Oh, I'll soften her up presently, you'll see Or else we could kidnap her. Bit of a shame though, if the monster eats her, quite a pretty girl—
FEVER. All for a crummy old book.
GRITTY. Mind you, I've been chatting up the locals down in the port, and there's legends about that crummy old book that would make a hard-boiled egg grow whiskers—
FEVER. Such as?
GRITTY. It's got all the secrets that's ever been wrote. Like how to make human beings, and go faster than light, and spin rhubarb and string vests out of the sun's rays—

FEVER [*thoughtfully*]. Handy kind of thing to have about.
          Seems a bit of a waste to pass it over to old
          Boss; he's got all he needs—
GRITTY [*singing*].
          Who doth not want a thing
             Except a place to sing
             And a fire to warm his feet
             In winter's wet and sleet,
          Give over, give over, give over,
             The book of all knowledge,
             As good as a college,
          Some know-how is better than fruitless en-
          deavor.
       [*During the song, SUNUP tiptoes out.*]
FEVER.   Where did Sunup go?
GRITTY.   Dunno—he was here just now. I wonder why
          Caliban doesn't use the book himself.
FEVER.   Maybe he doesn't need anything either. Or
          maybe he can't read. Sunup's pretty dumb,
          bit of a dead weight. If it weren't for him,
          you and I could split that four thousand be-
          tween us—
      [*GRITTY looks at him, rather startled.*]

SCENE FIVE

Hotel. LORD BOSS *flying kite.* SUNUP *enters conspiratorially
and follows him up and down as he plays string.*

SUNUP [*loud whisper*]. My lord! My lord! Hey, boss!

BOSS [*hearing him at last; annoyed*]. I didn't ask for you to come back. Well? What is it?

SUNUP. I thought as how you ought to know, boss, that that other precious pair. . . .

BOSS. Fever and Gritty?

SUNUP. Fever and Gritty are planning to play the old pitch-and-toss on you. That book you're so keen to get your hooks on—they're fixing to keep it for themselves. Well, stands to reason, dunnit? Read the book; you got all the power in the world—they'd be suckers if they handed it over, wouldn't they?

BOSS [*coolly*]. Well? And why are *you* being so honest and telling me this? Wouldn't they cut you in?

SUNUP [*virtuously*]. I wouldn't do you, boss—my lord. Not after all the long years I've worked for you. But I was thinking—if you'd like *me* to do the whole job—call them off, like—

BOSS. Then *you'd* get the whole four thousand, was that what you were thinking?

[SUNUP *nods, beaming.*]

And what's to stop *you* from doublecrossing me and keeping the book for yourself?

SUNUP. Why, what good would it be to me? I never learned to read, boss—anybody would tell you that—

[*The kite, an elaborate dragon/monster, suddenly flops out of the sky and lands on* SUNUP's *head as he and* LORD BOSS *stare measuringly at one another.*]

Scene Six

The lighthouse. RUTH *knitting.* FRED *wandering about with his Yo-Yo.*

RUTH.   Animal, vegetable, or mineral?
FRED.   You know I'm no good at intellectual games.
RUTH.   Please, Fred. It helps pass the time. I get so impatient, wondering when Sympathy will be here. Does the place look nice and welcoming?
FRED [*looking at cobwebs, shrugging*]. Yes. Fine. All right—animal.
RUTH.   On land?
FRED.   No.
RUTH.   In the air?
FRED.   No.
RUTH.   In the sea?
FRED.   Yes—I suppose so.
RUTH.   Within five miles of here?
FRED.   Yes.
RUTH.   Is it Caliban?
FRED.   See? You're too good at this game. . . . Yes.
RUTH.   Oh, dear. Fred? Do you think Caliban really exists? Sometimes I wonder if Saul hasn't just invented him. As an excuse for going down to the cave—
FRED [*with certainty*]. Oh, no. No. Caliban exists all right. I've been down there. I've seen him.

RUTH.   But why does Saul keep him shut up?

FRED.   Dunno. Dunno which of them is really the jailer. Maybe Caliban keeps Saul shut up.

RUTH.   What does he look like?

FRED.   It's hard to say.

RUTH.   D'you think he might ever get out and come up here?

[*They both look uneasily at the elevator.*]

        Fred! I can hear someone coming—it's Sympathy!

[RUTH *stands up, takes a few cautious steps toward the door.* SYMPATHY *opens it and rushes in.*]

SYMPATHY.   Mum! Mum! [*Runs to* RUTH *and hugs her.*]

RUTH.   Oh, dearie—I *am* pleased to see y— to have you back. [*Hugging her, running hands up arms, laying hand on top of head.*] You've grown so! My goodness, you must be nearly as tall as Dad—

SYMPATHY.   Why are you wearing dark glasses, Mum?

RUTH.   Oh—the light hurts my eyes a bit sometimes—it's nothing. But have you really finished at ballet school? Tell about your exams— did you do well?

SYMPATHY.   Yes, got a first class.

RUTH.   First class—that's wonderful! So now you're a real dancer—

SYMPATHY.   That's right. Want to see?

[SYMPATHY *starts doing ballet steps.* RUTH *is looking in the wrong direction.*]

SYMPATHY.   Mum! I'm over here.

[RUTH *obediently turns her head, but now* SYMPATHY *has moved again.*]

> No, *here*, love—

[RUTH *turns, still in the wrong direction;* SYMPATHY *stands watching her, more and more puzzled.*]

RUTH.   Where are you now, dearie?

SYMPATHY.   I'm here, Mum.

[SYMPATHY *now slowly surveys the interior and takes in the cobwebs and general muddle; beginning to suspect the truth, she moves silently up behind* RUTH *and extends her hand from behind in front of* RUTH'*s face.* RUTH *doesn't see it.* SYMPATHY *then gently puts her hands on* RUTH'*s shoulders.* RUTH *starts violently.*]

RUTH.   Oh—dearie—you startled me—

SYMPATHY [*with deep anxiety*]. Mum? Can't you see *at all?*

RUTH.   Well—no, darling—not really.

SYMPATHY.   So *that's* why you haven't answered my letters for so long. How long have you been bl— like this?

RUTH.   Oh—it took quite a while to come on—about five years.

SYMPATHY.   But didn't you go to a doctor?

RUTH.   You know how your father is about leaving this place—

SYMPATHY.   Just wait till I see Father and give him a piece of my mind—

RUTH.   Anyway, very likely a doctor wouldn't have been able to help. And I get on perfectly well.

SYMPATHY.   Yes, but—

RUTH.   I can knit socks for your father—and listen

	to the sea. You remember I always liked that best—
SYMPATHY.	But—
RUTH.	And I've got Fred and little Jenny for company—
SYMPATHY [*a little more cheerful*].	Oh, well, I'm glad they're still here. Where are they?
RUTH.	Why—right here—Fred was playing Twenty Questions with me just before you came. Weren't you, Fred—
FRED.	That's right. And she was beating me like she always does.
SYMPATHY [*puzzled*].	Fred's here? Where? I can't see him.
RUTH.	And little Jennet's in her cradle. She doesn't grow a bit, the angel; not like you, darling—
SYMPATHY [*really distressed*].	But I can't see her *either*! [*looking in cradle*] Oh, *nothing's* the way it should be.
RUTH [*sadly*].	I guess you've grown up, dearie—maybe that's why you can't see them anymore. Your father never could, you know—
SYMPATHY.	But you can—
RUTH.	Yes, but I'm blind.

FRED [*warningly*]. Here's Saul coming—

[*The elevator light has flashed green. Elevator music. Doors open with a puff of green smoke.*]

SAUL [*emerging from elevator with bucket*]. Something's definitely upsetting him—I don't like it.

[*He suddenly sees* SYMPATHY; *they stare at each other for a long, hostile pause.*]

Who are *you*?

RUTH.   Saul! It's your own daughter.

SYMPATHY.   As you perfectly well know.

SAUL [*putting down bucket, reaching for blunderbuss*].
               Now, look. I've said it before; I'm saying it
               again—I will not have you here. This is no
               place for—

SYMPATHY.   No place for children. *I* know. You said it
               before, and you got rid of me. But I'm not
               a child now—and I'm back and I'm staying.
               For as long as I choose. This is my *home*—

RUTH [*distressed*]. Oh, dearie! In a way he's right, you
               know—there won't be anything for you to
               do here. Your diploma for dancing will be
               just wasted.

SYMPATHY [*to* SAUL]. Why didn't you write and tell me
               she was going blind?

SAUL.   What was the use?

SYMPATHY.   Why didn't you take her to a doctor?

SAUL.   I knew it. I knew if you came home you'd
               start making trouble—

SYMPATHY.   You're just a selfish self-centered old *pig*—

SAUL.   I've got plenty of worries of my own. I
               haven't time to attend to your—

SYMPATHY.   Oh, I'm so angry I could *bash* you.

SAUL.   Clear out!

SYMPATHY.   Fancy letting your own wife go blind.

SAUL.   Go away! Get out of here!

SYMPATHY.   Not likely. *Look* at all this mess.

[*Ignoring* SAUL *and his blunderbuss, she snatches up a long
feather broom and starts whisking it about, narrowly miss-
ing* FRED'S *ghost who shrugs philosophically and keeps*

moving out of the way.]

You're not getting rid of me again—*some-body's* got to look after Mother—

RUTH. I don't really need looking after, you know, dearie.

SAUL [*more calmly, putting down gun, folding arms*]. You can't stay here. I need solitude.

SYMPATHY [*sweeping around his feet*]. Oh? And what do you need solitude *for?*

SAUL. To repent my crimes. This is a poisoned place.

SYMPATHY. Oh, that's right. I remember now. You used to go on like this before. So, okay, what's it poisoned by?

SAUL [*cunningly*]. If I tell you, will you clear out? And leave me and your mother in peace?

SYMPATHY. If I go I'll take her with me.

RUTH. Oh, lovey, I couldn't live anywhere but here—I'm used to this place.

SAUL. All right. I'll tell you if that'll get rid of you. I was a mooncusser.

[*From under a lot of cobwebs he drags out a large box which he has some difficulty in unlocking. He hoists up the stiff lid and takes out a number of miscellaneous objects, looks at them lovingly, and returns them to the box; they include a large painting, some mildewy bits of brocade, tarnished jewelry including a crown and scepter, a microscope, bits of machinery of whose use he is obviously ignorant, a molting fan, a helmet, archeological remains, etc. SYMPATHY watches, puzzled.*]

Act One, Scene Six

FRED [*singing, while* SAUL *opens the box*].
>When Force Twelve Gale doth loudly blow,
>And whirlpools whirl and glowworms glow,
>And birds sit brooding in the snow,
>And Gulf Stream reverseth towards Mexico,
>And Mother Carey's chicks are hatched,
>And mainsail do split and gotta be patched,
>>Hey ding-a-ding
>>We sing,
>For all events but ours are scratched.

SYMPATHY. A mooncusser? [*pause*] You mean a wrecker?

SAUL. I used to hang a bit of sacking over the light-house lamp. And then light a flare half a mile farther along the cliff, so ships would steer towards it and split themselves on Sabertooth Rock. [*beating his breast*] Many and many's the vessel that I've sent to the bottom in the old days.

SYMPATHY. And this old junk's what you got off the ships?

SAUL. Things that used to get washed up on Saber-tooth Rock.

SYMPATHY. What a collection of useless stuff.

SAUL. Oh, what an evil trade mine was! I shall never atone for it.

SYMPATHY [*thoughtfully*]. No, I don't see how you *can*. You must have finished off a lot of people who never did you any harm.

SAUL. Scores.

SYMPATHY. Why did you stop?

39

SAUL.   It was after I married your mother.

SYMPATHY.   Yes, I wouldn't think *she'd* stand for it.

RUTH.   He didn't tell me about it, dearie—not till the end.

SAUL.   It was sinking Fred's ship brought me up short.

FRED [*patiently*]. You *know* I don't hold it against you, Saulie—

SYMPATHY.   *You* sank Fred's boat? Your own brother?

SAUL.   My own brother.

SYMPATHY.   On purpose?

SAUL [*irritably*]. No, no, of course, not on purpose. He was a free-trader—

SYMPATHY.   You mean a smuggler?

SAUL.   The thing was, he didn't usually operate around here. Farther south was his run. How was I to know he'd be up this way? He was doing a special job for one of those professors at the university—fetching back art treasures from abroad.

SYMPATHY.   But didn't you recognize his ship?

SAUL.   It was at night, thick head.

SYMPATHY.   So what did you get from that haul?

SAUL.   Oh, how can you ask such a heartless question?

SYMPATHY.   I just wondered what there was on board.

SAUL.   It was a lot of historical stuff dredged up from the bottom of the Mediterranean. Some other government was laying claim to it. The most important thing was a book the professor wanted.

SYMPATHY.   What happened to the professor?

SAUL.   He was on board. He was drowned, too. They all were. My own brother! And his child. [*with a sudden access of guilt*] I killed them. Oh, what a wicked, wicked man I am.

SYMPATHY.   Is it wickeder to kill your own brother than anyone else?

SAUL [*shocked*]. Your own family? Of course it is.

FRED.   *Honest*, Saul, I know you didn't mean to do me in.

SYMPATHY [*indignantly*]. So just because you felt bad about killing Uncle Fred, you kept *me* away from my home all these years. Why should *I* be the one to suffer? What good did *that* do?

SCENE SEVEN

The cliff top. LORD BOSS *is bouncing about on a space-hopper painted like a globe, beside an elaborate tent.* SUNUP *comes in on tiptoe.*

SUNUP [*conspiratorially*]. Boss! Me lord!

BOSS [*looking at watch*]. Just a minute. Ten, nine, eight, seven, six, five, four, three, two, one, zero. [*He bounces as he counts.*] [*Distant explosion*]

SUNUP [*anxiously*]. What was that, Boss? You didn't blow up the lighthouse?

41

BOSS.   No, the hotel. I told them they knew what to expect if the tea was cold once more. You'll have to find me another hotel.

SUNUP.   There isn't any other hotel around here, my lord.

BOSS.   Then you'll have to finish the job today. Why are you here anyway? Have you got the book?

SUNUP.   No.

BOSS [*irritably*]. Go and get on with the job then.

SUNUP.   But I will. Look, I've found someone what's never told a lie. [*He pulls on the end of a long cord that he is holding, and a large red-and-blue bird waddles in.*]

BOSS [*unimpressed*]. *That?* What is it?

SUNUP [*proudly*]. It's a macaw. His name's Macawmack. He's never told a lie—have you, Mackie?

MACAWMACK. Keep off the grass. Give way. Trespassers will be persecuted. Penalty, five pounds. No smoking.

SUNUP.   You see? He couldn't tell a lie if he tried. Could you, Mackie? But he cost a bomb, Boss; I'll need some more expenses.

BOSS [*not pleased*]. How much?

MACAWMACK. No litter. No parking. Don't lean out of the window. Dogs must not foul this footway.

SUNUP [*shouting in* MACAWMACK's *ear*]. Sssh! [*to* BOSS] Three hundred.

[BOSS *reluctantly goes into tent.*]

SUNUP [*calling after him*]. And I'll need to borrow one of

42

your condensed-air guns, me lord. Getting
into the lighthouse is going to be tricky.

BOSS [*coming out with elaborate weapon and bundle of
notes*]. Well, hurry up, will you? The
weather's deteriorating. I'm not prepared to
hang about here much longer.

[*Sky darkens, wind whistles, loud peal of thunder. The tent
blows away.*]

SCENE EIGHT

Another part of the cliff top. FEVER *and* GRITTY *are hud-
dling under large umbrella.*

FEVER.   I don't think much of *your* plan. At this rate
we're likely to be washed over the cliff before
we ever get into the lighthouse.

GRITTY.   For heaven's sake! Where's your subtlety?
You've got to use subtlety with girls. I just
laid a little posy with a photo of a dolphin
on the lighthouse doorstep. That'll remind
her of me.

FEVER [*disgustedly*]. A posy! Why should a dolphin remind
her of you? You don't look like a dolphin.

GRITTY.   Forget-me-nots and sea lavender and dol-
phiniums.

FEVER.   Did you see her?

GRITTY.   No, but she's bound to come out sometime
to take in the milk.

FEVER.   How do you know they have milk delivered?
I've never seen a milkman go up. Maybe they
keep a goat.

GRITTY.   Then she'll go out to milk the goat.

FEVER.   In my opinion we'd better just blast our way
in. I pinched one of the boss's condensed-air
guns—thought it might come in handy—

GRITTY.   Don't you see, you triple-distilled fool, if you
do that, then old Whiskers will pull the lever
that topples over the rock that smashes the
wreck, and we'll *never* get the flaming book?
No. Patience is the only answer.
          [*sings*]
Tell me where is Patience mustered,
How can you stop from getting flustered,
How remain as cool as custard?
You must learn to meditate,
Don't be so precipitate,
Everything comes to chaps as wait,
Play it by ear, work to rule,
Whatever happens, keep your cool,
Keep your cool.
[SYMPATHY *comes running in.*]

SYMPATHY [*breathless*]. Oh, I'm so glad you're still here.
I was afraid you might have left.

GRITTY [*triumphant glance at* FEVER]. There, what did I
tell you?
          [*To* SYMPATHY] Did you find my posy?

44

SYMPATHY.   Posy? No. What posy?

    [FEVER *returns* GRITTY's *glance.*]

    No, I came to ask you—to ask you to help me—

GRITTY.   Anything we can do, of course—oh, this is my mate—

SYMPATHY [*hasty nod to* FEVER]. Pleased to meet you. [*to* GRITTY] You did say—you said you had plenty of money—

GRITTY.   Sure. At least we haven't actually got the cash on us, but we can get it from this chap who's giving us our grant—

FEVER.   Grant? What grant?

    [GRITTY *gives him warning kick.*]

SYMPATHY.   You see, my mother's gone blind—I want to get her to a doctor, but I've no money for the fee—

GRITTY [*easily*]. Yeah, we could help you with that. Take you and your mum into town on the bike, if you like.

SYMPATHY.   Oh, that's kind of you—and I'll try to help you with your research.

FEVER.   Research?

GRITTY.   Yes, if we could just get a quick look at the dolphin first.

FEVER.   Dolphin?

    [GRITTY *scowls at him.*]

SYMPATHY.   Yes, I've been thinking about that—I've got a sort of plan what to do. After all, it isn't as if it was Dad's dolphin—it doesn't seem

	fair he should stop you from looking at it just because he used to be a mooncusser and says the place is poisoned—
FEVER.	Poisoned?
SYMPATHY.	So I thought I could let you in very quietly while Dad's upstairs polishing the lamp—
GRITTY.	Fine.
SYMPATHY.	Then I'll go up and start arguing with him so as to keep him out of the way while you go down in the elevator—Dad loves arguing, he'll do that for hours.
GRITTY.	Won't you come down, too, and see the dolphin?
FEVER [*simultaneously with* GRITTY].	We'd like you to come with us.
GRITTY.	Besides, you'll need to show us how to work the elevator.
SYMPATHY.	Oh, that's easy. It's electronically controlled. You sing a tune to make the doors open. It was my dad's invention.
FEVER.	Sing a tune?
SYMPATHY.	Yes, he changes it every month. Just now it goes like this.
	[*She hums elevator music.*]
GRITTY.	In that case you'll definitely have to come with us. My mate's tone-deaf, and I can never carry a tune in my head—suppose we forgot it when we was down there—
SYMPATHY [*taken aback*].	Oh. Well, we'll have to think of some plan to keep Dad out of the way then.
GRITTY.	That shouldn't be too difficult.

46

[*He ushers* SYMPATHY *out under umbrella while behind them* FEVER *pulls out a condensed-air gun and cocks it.*]

SCENE NINE

The lighthouse. Remains of meal on table: teapot, loaf.
SAUL *has constructed a trap to catch anyone coming through the door. It is a cage made of string and wicker, has a sliding trapdoor that drops down at one side. He is putting finishing touches on it, trying to get the slide to stay up. It keeps falling down. At present, the cage—which is on casters—is in the middle of the room. Knock at outer door. Trapdoor falls again.*

SAUL [*crossly, over his shoulder*]. Wait, I'm not ready yet—
[*But the door opens.* LORD BOSS *and* SUNUP *come in.*]
SAUL [*angrily*]. Who are you? Get out. I never said you
could come in. Get out, I tell you!
BOSS.   We're from the Ministry.
SAUL.   What Ministry?
BOSS.   Ministry of Frontiers, Boundaries, and Mysteries.
SAUL.   I'll have no snoopers here.
BOSS.   We have a trained macaw, licensed to locate marsh gas, fire damp, poltergeists, atmospheric pollution, and psychic phenomena.
SAUL.   Get out.
BOSS.   We've heard you're infested with ghosts here; we have an order to inspect.

SAUL.   I order you to clear out.

[SUNUP *hauls on cord;* MACAWMACK *waddles in, looking very dejected.*]

SUNUP.   Ah, have a heart; our hotel just fell into the sea.

SAUL.   You can go and jump after it for all I care.

BOSS.   And it's raining cats and dogs.

SAUL.   One step farther and I shoot.

[*Snatches up blunderbuss, pulls trigger but misses, dislodges large mass of cobwebs which falls on him and the gun.*]

SUNUP [*gazing at the cage*]. What the dickens is that?

SAUL [*struggling out from under cobwebs; the gun is still hopelessly entangled*]. It's a daughter-catcher.

SUNUP.   How does it work?

SAUL.   Simple. My daughter's outside somewhere at the moment. I wheel it up to the door.

SUNUP.   And she walks in?

SAUL.   Straight into the trap. The slide falls; then I just wheel it outside with her in it.

SUNUP.   I don't see how the sliding bit works.

SAUL.   Like this. [*But when he turns to demonstrate,* SUNUP *shoots him with condensed-air gun, which makes a noise like water running out of a basin. He falls, stunned.*]

BOSS.   I *said* it would be easy. Why do I always end up on the job myself? Is he dead?

SUNUP [*examining*]. No. D'you want him dead?

BOSS.   Not yet. We might need him to show us how to get down to the cave.

[*They dump him on armchair, cover him with drape of cobweb.*]

48

SUNUP [*looking around*]. That must be the elevator. But there doesn't seem to be a call button.

BOSS.   Maybe it's on the next floor. Go up and see.

[SUNUP *goes upstairs to gallery, and then through door. MACAWMACK thoughtfully inspects cage and clambers in. The trap falls and shuts him in.*]

MACAWMACK [*dolefully*]. No exit. No way through. No way out!

BOSS.   It's your own fault, you stupid bird. *I'm* not going to let you out. [*He pokes* MACAWMACK *with a bit of cane.* MACAWMACK *pecks back like lightning, and he only just leaps out of the way in time.*] You can just wait till Sunup gets back. Hey! [*calling upstairs*] Have you found another entrance? Hurry up, the old guy will be coming to before long.

SUNUP [*reappearing on gallery*]. There's a woman asleep up here, me lord—

BOSS.   Never mind her. Have you found any doors?

SUNUP [*doubtfully*]. Nothing that looks like elevator doors. I haven't been right up to the top of the tower—they say there's one thousand, two hundred and ninety-eight steps.

BOSS.   I suppose I'll have to come—you wouldn't recognize the Atlantic Ocean if you found it in your kitchen sink. [*He follows* SUNUP.]

MACAWMACK [*furiously battering at the cage*]. No parking, no lurking, no loitering, no smoking, no waiting, no skating, no talking, no boating, no joking. SILENCE, OPERATION IN PROGRESS!

SCENE TEN

Same scene as previous. Enter SYMPATHY [*in the lead*], GRITTY, *and* FEVER.

SYMPATHY [*seeing* SAUL *lying in armchair*]. Sssh, Dad's asleep. That's a bit of luck.

GRITTY [*seeing* MACAWMACK *in cage*]. What's *that?*

SYMPATHY.   Pet of Dad's, I suppose.

FEVER.   Never mind him. Where's the elevator?

SYMPATHY.   Those doors.

FEVER.   Let's have the tune then, miss—

GRITTY.   Yeah, let's get down there while the coast's clear.

SYMPATHY.   Um—[*She stands looking blankly ahead of her.*] Pom, pom, pom, pom—no, that's not it; la, la, la, no; tiddle tiddle tum—I almost had it then. Oh, this is so *stupid;* ten minutes ago I had it in my head clear as "God Save the Queen."

FEVER.   You've gone and forgotten it?

SYMPATHY.   It'll come back—I'm sure it will. It's a tune I know quite well.

FEVER.   Yeah, and in the meantime old Whiskers there will wake up.

GRITTY.   What about your mum? Wouldn't she know the tune?

SYMPATHY.   That's a good idea. She must be upstairs

50

having her nap—I'll take her a cup of tea.
[*She pours a cup from pot on table and goes upstairs and through gallery door.*]

MACAWMACK. Self-service only. Mind the step. Use this door. *Don't* use this door. All tickets to be shown. Look out for the platform. Put coin in slot.

GRITTY. Oh, be quiet. No one asked you to speak.

FEVER. Maybe we could get the elevator doors open.

[*He tries to pry them apart; a little green smoke comes out.*]

GRITTY [*nervously*]. Hey, watch it; you might electrocute yourself. Anyway it's no use if the elevator isn't on this floor.

MACAWMACK. Beds, bedding, bathroom, and all soft furnishings.

GRITTY. I've an idea. I'll try and get in touch with Caliban; he ought to know the tune— [*He pulls out pocket radio transmitter, switches on.*]

Hello, hello, hello, Caliban. Are you there, Caliban? Calling Caliban. Caliban, can you hear me, Caliban? Calling Caliban—

[*His back is turned; he doesn't see* RUTH *coming downstairs, starts violently when she comes silently into his field of vision.* SYMPATHY *follows, running down with empty cup, guides* RUTH *to her rocking chair.*]

SYMPATHY. You okay, Mum? Can I get you anything?

RUTH. No, dearie, thank you. Where's your father?

SYMPATHY. He seems to be asleep.

RUTH. At this time of day? That's funny.

SYMPATHY. Let's not disturb him.

RUTH. Isn't there somebody else here?

SYMPATHY. Oh—er—yes, it's—er—two friends of mine, Mum.

RUTH. What are their names?

[SYMPATHY *looks inquiringly at them; they murmur their names and she repeats.*]

SYMPATHY. Gritty and Fever, Mum—this is my mother.

RUTH. How do you do?

FEVER *and* GRITTY [*together, a little embarrassed*]. Pleased to meet you, ma'am.

RUTH. I'm afraid your father won't be pleased when he wakes, dear. He doesn't like visitors at all.

SYMPATHY. They needn't stay long.

RUTH. Where did you meet your friends?

SYMPATHY. Outside—just now.

RUTH. Before that, I meant. Were they at ballet school with you?

SYMPATHY. Er—yes.

RUTH. Just fancy; so you're both dancers; did you get your diplomas at the same time as Sympathy?

GRITTY. That's right. [*He strikes a ballet posture, not being sure if* RUTH *can see anything or not.*]

FEVER [*who has been growing very impatient*]. Ma'am—we were wondering if you could help us with the tune that gets this elevator working. Your daughter said she would but she's forgotten it—

52

Scene Eleven

The lamp room. Sunup *and* Lord Boss *totter in, exhausted from climbing all those stairs.* Fred's *ghost, surprised but pleased to see them, is already there.*

Fred [*singing*].
> Come unto this rockbound coast,
> Every ghost;
> Any spook who turns up here
> Gets a beer;
> Welcome, welcome to our shore,
> There's always room for just one more.
>> Hark, hark,
>> Peek-a-boo
>> The owls do bark,
>> To-wit-to-woo.
>> Hark, hark, I hear
>> Dolphins singing far and near,
>> A.E.I.O.U.

[Sunup *and* Boss, *insensibly influenced, begin to stagger about like zombies, then slowly subside into meditation posture and sit staring ahead of them.* Fred's *ghost strolls out.*]

SCENE TWELVE

The lighthouse. Same as Scene Ten. FRED's *ghost strolls downstairs.*

FRED.   Company, I see. Fancy meeting up with old Fever again.

RUTH [*surprised*]. Do you know them, Fred?

FRED.   The old one, I do; he used to be on the Yucatan straw-hat run with me in the old days.

RUTH.   That's queer; he's a classmate of Sympathy's; you'd think he'd be rather too old for a ballet student.

FRED.   Old Fever a ballet student? You might as well teach a stalagmite to play hopscotch.

GRITTY [*to* SYMPATHY; *low voice*]. Is your mum all right? She's talking to herself.

SYMPATHY.   She's talking to Uncle Fred's ghost.

FEVER [*in despair*]. Gawdamighty—ghosts, monsters, parrots—nutty old guys with whiskers—this is the screwiest job I ever was on—

RUTH.   Your friends want to go down in the elevator, dear, is that it, to the cave?

SYMPATHY.   Yes, they're studying dolphins.

RUTH.   Dolphins?

SYMPATHY.   They want to—to make up a ballet about dolphins.

RUTH.   But there aren't any dolphins down in the cave—only Caliban.

SYMPATHY.   Caliban? [*puzzled*] Who's Caliban? [*to* GRITTY] You were calling Caliban, Caliban, just now when I came downstairs—is Caliban the dolphin's name?

RUTH.   No, Caliban's not a dolphin, lovey; he's something your father keeps down there in the cave.

SYMPATHY.   A *person?* You mean Father's got someone shut in down there?

RUTH.   No, not a person—I'm not sure what he is.

SYMPATHY.   But why's he there?

RUTH.   Your father says there's an old book down there, sealed up in a lead box. Caliban thinks it belongs to him—

SYMPATHY.   You mean to say, Father's pinched a book he's no right to, and he's got the real owner shut up down there—

RUTH.   I believe he did once say he'd give it back, but then he changed his mind—he said it would only lead to trouble—

SYMPATHY.   Isn't that just *like* Father—he's got no *right* to keep it. [*She starts toward* SAUL, *as if to shake him awake, but then an idea strikes her, and she turns to* GRITTY. Hey—did *you* know all this?

GRITTY [*embarrassed*]. Well—

FEVER [*impatient*]. Go on—tell her it's the book we're after.

SYMPATHY.   You've been fooling me, haven't you? [*furi-*

ous] And I *liked* you—I really thought you wanted to help Mum and me. You've just been telling me *lies*—you and your dolphins' dreams.

GRITTY [*injured*]. Well, I *would* have helped you—anyway you've no call to act so superior; you've been telling lies yourself. [*Suddenly realizes the implication of this.*] Oh, no. . . . [*He stares at* SYMPATHY *aghast, and pulls the wrapped ball out of his pocket.*] Here, hold this again for a moment, will you. . . . [*Puzzled, she takes it.*] Anyway—so we *do* want the book—it certainly doesn't belong to your dad.

FEVER. And you do want to get your mum to a doctor.

RUTH. Dearie, I didn't realize that was what you were planning. I don't think it would be any use at all—a doctor can't help me now.

SYMPATHY [*screaming*]. Oh, it's hot—why didn't you warn me? [*She drops the ball, which bounces into* RUTH'*s lap.*]

FEVER [*sourly to* GRITTY]. Now look what you've done; you've properly loused things up.

CALIBAN'S VOICE [*coming through amplified on* GRITTY'*s transmitter*]. Help, help, help, this is Caliban! Help me, help me. Let me out of here. It's dark; I'm lonely! Please, please, send someone to help me. Send me someone who's never told a lie—

[*There is an awestruck silence.*]

RUTH [*thoughtfully, half to herself*]. I could go and let that poor creature out.

SYMPATHY.   No, Mum! He might be dangerous. You're not to!

FRED.   He's got a very nasty temper, Ruthie, after being shut up all this time—I'd leave the job to someone else.

GRITTY.   *Would* you do it, ma'am?

SYMPATHY.   *No!*

FEVER.   Look, we're all arguing—let's get the flaming elevator up, eh? Can you sing us the tune, Mum.

RUTH.   Oh, dear. Saul keeps changing it. Let's think now, is it the one that goes to Dublin's fair city? [*She sings "Cockles and Mussels," but it isn't*]. It has something to do with the sea this month, I know—

SYMPATHY.   "Blow the Wind Southerly"? [*She tries.*]

GRITTY.   "What Shall We Do with the Drunken Sailor"? [*He has a go.*]

FEVER.   "Oh, I Do Like to Be Beside the Seaside"? [*He joins in.*]

MACAWMACK. Lower the boats! Fire, fire! Avast the main brace! Women and children first! Crew members only!

[*At last he succeeds in raising the sliding door of the cage and clambers out, very excited; FEVER and GRITTY back away from him, still singing; but SYMPATHY tosses him the loaf from the table, which he takes briskly.*]

GRITTY *and* FEVER *together* [*changing their tune*].
> The master, the swabber, the bosun and I,
> The gunner and his mate
> Loved Moll, Meg, Marian, and Margery,
> But none of us cared for Kate.

[SAUL *rouses up at all this noise, staggers a few steps toward the cage, and falls forward into it; the shutter falls again.*]

BOSS [*entering above on gallery, pointing gun*]. Keep quite
> still, the lot of you. Put your hands above
> your heads.

[*He yawns, still shaking off* FRED'*s influence; so does* SUNUP, *who has followed him in. Everyone puts hands over head.* SUNUP *and* BOSS *come down. They have large plastic manacles like the rosette-type wall fixtures that towels and teacloths are hung from; they simply jam one of these over each pair of hands. At this moment* SYMPATHY *by chance hits on the right tune, and the elevator music begins playing; light glows green. As the last pair of hands is secured, doors come open with a cloud of green smoke.*]

BOSS.
> Sunup, get that bird into the lift. We'll take
> the girl, too—come on you [*to* SYMPATHY;
> *he pushes her into the lift and turns to say*]
> You'd better all keep quiet up here, or I don't
> guarantee to bring the girl back with us.
> > [*Elevator doors close.*]
> > [CURTAIN]

ACT TWO

SCENE ONE

The cave. Long green filaments hanging from ceiling. Rocks here and there on the ground and a rock shelf at rear. Large bottle partially visible at one side, neck and huge cork protruding, with part of ship visible inside. Elevator doors at rear as in lighthouse.

Doors open. LORD BOSS, SYMPATHY, *still with hands fastened,* SUNUP, *and* MACAWMACK *emerge. Elevator music. Doors close.*

SUNUP.   Creepus, what a spooky hole! I don't like it down here, Boss. I'm scared.

BOSS.   Oh, don't be so wet. What's going to hurt you?

[A large crab clambers over his foot; he jumps back.]

MACAWMACK *[sepulchrally]*. Private fishing. Bathing strictly forbidden. No landing. Dangerous undertow.

SUNUP *[irritably]*. Oh, do be quiet. You're no help at all. *[looking around]* Where d'you suppose Caliban is then? He *asked* us to come down here—why don't he come out and say hello?

BOSS.   I daresay he's not far off. *[calling]* Caliban! Caliban! Where are you?

SUNUP, SYMPATHY, *and* BOSS *[together]*. Caliban, Caliban, Caliban!

ECHO.   Caliban, ibaniban, iban, iban, ban ban, ban. . . .

SUNUP [*uneasily*]. Maybe that voice we heard over the transmitter was just an echo all along.

BOSS.   Rubbish. Don't be stupid. You heard it answer, didn't you? It said things; it didn't just echo. Caliban, where are you? Why don't you come out? We've brought you someone who's never told a lie.

ECHO.   Aye, aye, aye, aye, aye. . . .

SYMPATHY.   Oh, it's horrible here; it gives me the shivers. How *could* Father keep someone shut up down here? Caliban, *do* come out. We're all waiting for you.

MACAWMACK. Bring out your dead, bring out your dead!

SUNUP.   Quiet, you stupid bird. Boss, I've had a thought. Maybe Caliban's shut up somewhere. Maybe he's inside the bottle.

BOSS.   First sensible thought you've had since I've known you. Maybe he is.

SYMPATHY [*shivering*]. How're we going to get him out, then?

SUNUP.   Break the bottle, I suppose. [*He bangs the bottle with his gun; no result.*]

BOSS.   Why not pull out the cork?

[LORD BOSS *and* SUNUP *try to pull out cork without success.*]

SUNUP.   We might try bashing the cork with a big stone.

[*He starts wandering about, looking for a suitable stone.*]

SYMPATHY [*studying the cork*]. There's words written on the cork.

SUNUP.   I know. [*after a pause*] What does it say?

SYMPATHY.   Can't you read?

SUNUP.   No. Can't you?

SYMPATHY.   Well, yes—I can read English—but this is some foreign language, even the letters are peculiar.

[LORD BOSS *produces flashlight and shines it.*]

SYMPATHY.   Can you move the light this way? Thanks— Uligarr—something—I'm not sure if that's right. Yes, Uligarra-Zalgarra, that's it: Uligarra-Zalgarra. I wonder what it means? Oh—

[*With a tremendous amplified noise of glass breaking, the bottle disintegrates and the cork shoots out; explosion light-effect. In the middle of all this,* CALIBAN *emerges. He is like a green gorilla, furry, with gills and webfeet; his expression is both sad and malevolent.*]

SUNUP.   Blimey, what a smell of fish.

BOSS.   Are—are you Caliban?

CALIBAN.   Are you dirty water, are you coal dust? Are you mud, are you offal, are you sweepings?

BOSS.   Certainly not. My name is no affair of yours.

CALIBAN.   And *my* name is my own affair. Caliban is what they call me, but Caliban is not my real name.

SUNUP.   Well, there's no call to put on airs with us. What is your real name then?

CALIBAN [*cunningly*].   Aha! That I shan't tell you, or it would give you power over me.

BOSS.   Oh, very well. Have it your own way.

CALIBAN.   I *intend* to have it my own way.

BOSS.   There's no need to take that tone with us. We've come to help you,

CALIBAN. How do I know that? No one has ever helped me. How do I know you're telling the truth?

BOSS. What would be the point of lying to you? We've come all this way on purpose to do you a good turn—

CALIBAN. The other one lied to me. He promised to use the book and then let me go. If he had used the book, it would have set me free. But he lied. He never used it, and he never freed me. He broke his promise.

SYMPATHY. That was my dad, I suppose. Sounds like him.

CALIBAN [*shouting, wagging his head from side to side, beating on his chest*]. Flout'em and scout'em and scout'em and flout'em. Ahhhhh! I hate you all, hate you, hate you, hate you!

[*He jumps towards them furiously, and they scatter in fright.*]

SYMPATHY. But *we* haven't done anything bad to you, Caliban. Why do you hate us? We've come here to help you.

CALIBAN. I don't believe you. You're all liars.

BOSS. That's not so. We'll *show* you that we're not liars. Only tell us where the book's kept—

SUNUP [*low voice to* LORD BOSS]. Suppose he don't know?

CALIBAN. Why should I tell you? Why should I give my secrets away?

BOSS [*impatiently*]. Oh, good heavens, what an oaf. Look here—we brought you someone who's never told a lie.

CALIBAN. I don't believe you.

BOSS. It's the absolute, stone-cold, grass-green,

home-ground truth. That bird there has never told a lie in his life.

CALIBAN. I hate you, hate you, hate you.

SYMPATHY. Why do you hate us, Caliban?

CALIBAN. Because there's a whole world full of you—and there's only one of me.

BOSS. That's not our fault.

CALIBAN. Once the world was full of Calibans—now I'm all alone and I'm lonely, lonely, lonely—and you're all packed tight like rats.

BOSS. Just hand over the book, and I'll make twenty more Calibans just like you—a hundred—*five* hundred, if you like—then you'll never be lonely again.

SUNUP [*low voice*]. Strewth, what a prospect. . . . Hey, Boss, you don't really mean to do that?

BOSS [*low voice*]. Of course not. Don't be more of a fool than you can help.

SUNUP. Why don't he use the book himself?

BOSS. Maybe he's like you—can't read. He doesn't seem very bright.

SYMPATHY [*to* CALIBAN]. Honestly, the bird doesn't tell lies. You could talk to him.

CALIBAN [*surlily addressing* MACAWMACK]. Where can I find another me? Where can I find Caliban's mate?

MACAWMACK [*after considerable thought*]. Press Button B and get your money back.

CALIBAN. Treachery! Betrayal! I can see into your black hearts. You just mean to mock me. You thought you could steal Caliban's book and

66

leave him alone in the dark. Didn't you? Didn't you? But you won't be able to use it, and I'll never give it to you—never, never, never, never.

SYMPATHY. Oh, gosh, that really riled him. I'm scared. [*She turns and notices* FRED, *who has come in behind her.*] Uncle Fred! How did you get here? I never heard the elevator.

FRED. I don't need to use the elevator like you lot; I can come down whenever I fancy. Only I don't often fancy. But your mum asked me to drop down and see was you all right; she was getting nervous about you.

SYMPATHY. *I'm* getting nervous about me. What'll Caliban do, Uncle Fred?

FRED. I don't rightly know. I always did think your Dad was silly to keep him shut up. Now he's got out of his bottle, who's to say? Best climb up here, out of harm's way.

SYMPATHY. Could you get this thing off my hands, Uncle Fred?

FRED. Sorry, love, I can't manage that.

SYMPATHY. Well, could you sing the elevator music? I can't; my t-t-teeth are ch-ch-chattering s-s-so.

FRED. I never was any good at getting electrical things to work. [*He tries but nothing happens.*] I daresay Caliban's jammed it.

[SYMPATHY *scrambles up on rock ledge beside him; meanwhile* CALIBAN *is making darting attacks on* LORD BOSS *and* SUNUP, *which they dodge.*]

SYMPATHY. How is it I can see you, Uncle Fred, when
I couldn't before?

FRED. I daresay you're in a state of shock.

CALIBAN [*to* LORD BOSS *and* SUNUP]. You think you're so
wonderful because you can *think*. Where
has thinking got you? Do you think you can
get the better of me?

MACAWMACK [*who has retreated to the shelf with* FRED
and SYMPATHY]. Danger! Keep away from
live rail. Thirty thousand volts. Poison. High
explosive. High tension. Don't touch.

SUNUP [*dodging attack by* CALIBAN]. Boss! For heaven's
sake! Why don't you shoot him?

BOSS. And lose my chance of finding the book?

[*Loud crash; colored lights shoot upwards; dark.*]

SCENE TWO

The lighthouse. GRITTY *is standing beside* FEVER, *jumping
up and down so as to dislodge* FEVER's *manacles with his
head. He finally succeeds.* FEVER *takes* GRITTY's *manacles
off.* GRITTY *takes* RUTH's *off.*

RUTH. Thank you.

GRITTY. Would you like a cup of tea, ma'am?

RUTH [*faintly*]. That would be nice. You'll find tea in the
blue tin.

GRITTY.   Make some tea, Fever. There's a good guy.
[He goes to elevator doors and sings elevator tune over and over; nothing happens.]
Why won't the blasted elevator come up?

FEVER *[making tea]*. Maybe it's jammed. Maybe Caliban's done something to it down at the bottom. Maybe Boss left the doors open. Anyway— d'you *want* to go down?

GRITTY *[low voice]*. I feel bad about the girl.

FEVER.   Dunno why. *You* were going to take her down yourself in the first place.

GRITTY.   I know. But just the same I feel bad.

RUTH.   Where's my husband?

[SAUL, inside the cage, has just come to, staggered upright, shaken off drapery of cobwebs, and started furiously rattling the bars.]

SAUL.   Let me out, let me out, let me out.

FEVER.   Oh, all right.

[FEVER undoes the sliding door. SAUL bounds out of the cage and rushes to a large lever on the wall, which he pulls; there is a muffled distant explosion; SAUL then goes upstairs without taking any further notice of anybody.]

GRITTY *[despairingly]*. Now you *have* done it.

FEVER.   Done what?

GRITTY.   Don't you see, you dumb fool? That was the lever that releases the rock that smashes the ship.

FEVER.   Oh. . . . *[slowly taking it in]* You mean he's smashed up Boss and all below there.

GRITTY.   Almost certainly.

69

FEVER.   Ask me, that's not a bad thing; Boss and
            Sunup's no loss.
GRITTY.   What about the girl? [FEVER *has made tea,
            hands him a cup; absently he passes it to
            RUTH.*] Here's your tea, ma'am.
RUTH.   Thank you.
GRITTY.   You've no call to thank us, ma'am; all we've
            done is bring trouble—your daughter's down
            in the cave with that monster—and Boss and
            Sunup, who aren't much better—let alone
            the fact that your husband has just pulled
            down a rock on them.
RUTH.   Oh, it may not be too bad; I asked my broth-
            er-in-law's ghost to go down and keep an eye
            on her.
GRITTY.   I don't see what a *ghost* can do. Ma'am, is
            there any other way of getting down to the
            cave, apart from the elevator, which seems
            to be stuck?
RUTH [*dubiously*]. You could climb down the cliff, I sup-
            pose. Then it rather depends how close the
            whirlpool is—it moves up and down the
            channel. Sometimes you can get past it,
            sometimes not.
GRITTY.   Oh, well, I might have a go. Here. . . . [*He
            picks up long coil of rope, shakes off cob-
            webs, fastens one end around his middle, and
            passes an end to* FEVER.] Just tie that round
            the stair rail, will you? And do a clove hitch,
            none of your grannies. I'm going to have a

bash at going down the cliff. See you at sup-
pertime, I hope. [*He climbs out the window.*]

[FEVER *thoughtfully considers the rope he is holding. He
ties it to the stair rail. Waits for a few minutes, then,
equally thoughtfully, takes the bread knife from the table
and saws through the rope. Loud amplified twang! Distant
splash.*]

SCENE THREE

The cave. SYMPATHY, FRED, *and* MACAWMACK *still on the
ledge.*

SYMPATHY.   My goodness, Uncle Fred, I *am* pleased you
              came down to keep us company. What do
              you think happened to the others?

FRED.   I think that rock fell on them. [*He points
              to large rock occupying the spot where
              ship-in-bottle was before.*] In fact, I can see
              their feet sticking out.

SYMPATHY.   Oh, dear. Caliban, too?

FRED.   I can't see his feet. I rather think when the
              rock fell on those two, he got shot upwards;
              but I don't know where he is.

SYMPATHY.   Poor Caliban.

FRED.   Don't waste your sympathy on him; he's got
              a thoroughly disagreeable nature.

SYMPATHY.   He's had a rotten deal, though. Suppose you'd been shut up all that time?

FRED.   I wouldn't have minded; I'd have been a bit more pleasant about it.

SYMPATHY.   Oh, Uncle Fred, how are we going to get out of here?

FRED.   I dunno.

SYMPATHY.   Macawmack, can't you say something useful?

MACAWMACK. Hold on tight. Have all fares ready, please. No dogs allowed. No children under fourteen. No musical instruments to be played in the subway.

SYMPATHY.   That's no help. I only wish we did have a musical instrument. At least we could cheer ourselves up. We'll have to do exercises to pass the time and keep warm.

[*She stands, starts doing exercises which turn to arabesques, then she is dancing as well as she can with tied hands.* FRED *joins in doing a hornpipe.* MACAWMACK *flaps his wings. When* FRED *tires of dancing he sings.*]

FRED [*singing*].

> When nights are black with mist and murk,
> That's when the mooncussers get to work,
> With pick and pike and spike and dirk
> Behind each rock a bloke doth lurk,
> And keels are split and hulls are stove
> And wrecks cast up in every cove.
>   Why then we sing
>   Hey ding-a-ding
> For this is the weather we approve.

SYMPATHY [*sinking exhausted on rock*]. This is a nice square rock. Hey—it has a lid. It's not a rock; it's a box—

FRED.   Does it open?

SYMPATHY [*struggles to open lid*]. Yes, it's coming.

FRED.   Anything inside? Pieces of eight?

SYMPATHY.   No, it's a book—it must be *Caliban's* book. Caliban—Caliban! Are you there? I found your book—

ECHO.   Ook, ook, ook, ook. . . .

FRED.   That's useful. If you can read even the first word, I reckon it'll get us out of here.

SYMPATHY.   Well, I can't open it. It's padlocked.

         [*Lights start to swing around and around.*]

SCENE FOUR

The lighthouse. RUTH *in rocking chair.* FEVER *looking out of window.* FEVER *turns and approaches* RUTH.

FEVER [*in official voice*]. Madam, I am an official from the Ministry of Frontiers, Boundaries, and Mysteries. I must inform you that we have been given to understand that your husband may be concealing stolen goods on these premises—namely a book of—um, historical value—and I have a warrant to search for it.

RUTH.   Oh, my goodness. Well—go on, search if you must—*I* can't stop you. But Saul won't be pleased. And, honestly, he gave up all that business *years* ago—I'm certain you won't find anything. Anyway, why don't you ask him? [*calling*] Saul! Saul!

[*Sky outside window has become very dark. Thunder and lightning.* CALIBAN *appears outside window in flash of lightning, climbs in under cover of following dark, and is then seen inside.* FEVER *sees him, is riveted with terror, then gives wild scream. He rushes for the window and jumps out. Loud amplified splash a moment or two later.*]

RUTH [*puzzled*]. What's the matter?

[CALIBAN *doesn't answer but stands with arms folded looking up the stairs.*]

RUTH.   Saul! Saul! Could you stop polishing and come down a moment? There's a man from the ministry here, and I think he must have hurt himself.

  [SAUL *comes out of door onto gallery.*]

SAUL [*irritable*]. Not *another?* I told the last lot to clear out.

[*He sees* CALIBAN, *is transfixed with terror, but compelled to come on down. He slowly and reluctantly descends stairs, approaches* CALIBAN, *struggling against the compulsion, and crouches on the ground in front of* CALIBAN *with arms over head.* CALIBAN, *who has gathered up a thick mat of black cobweb, drops it over him completely covering him.* SAUL *gradually shrinks under it until it lies flat on the floor.*]

RUTH.   Really I don't understand anything that's happening today. Saul? Are you there?

CALIBAN [*in* SAUL's *voice*]. Yes, I'm here.

RUTH.   Where's the man from the ministry?

CALIBAN.   He's gone.

RUTH.   Did he find the book he's looking for?

CALIBAN.   It isn't here.

RUTH [*relieved*]. I told him it wasn't; I said you'd given up all that business long ago. What's happened to all the other people who were here before? Sympathy's school friends and the bird and those other people?

CALIBAN.   Two of them are coming now.

[SUNUP *and* BOSS *come through the door, dressed in white versions of their previous costumes, with white faces like* FRED. *They seem dazed and confused.*]

SUNUP.   Strewth, what happened? Where are we?

BOSS.   I think we're in Rome airport. I want a first-class return to Pernambuco and a champagne cocktail.

SUNUP.   *I* don't think we're in Rome airport. I can't see any newsstands. And I can't see my feet. I'm scared.

RUTH.   Oh, you poor things. Don't you know what's happened to you?

           [*They stare at her blankly.*]

RUTH.   Well, at least you'll be company for Fred. Saul, could you pass me my knitting? I think it's on the table.

           [CALIBAN *does so.*]

SCENE FIVE

The cave. Tremendous whirl of lights to represent whirl-pool; they gradually slow down and come to a stop. GRITTY *drops down, reeling around and around, finally sinks to the ground.*

SYMPATHY [*who has been perched on rock, jumps off, and runs to him joyfully*]. Gritty! How ever did you get down here?

GRITTY. Well, I started climbing down the cliff—but when I was nearly at the bottom, the rope broke.

SYMPATHY. Heavens! You never fell through the whirl-pool?

GRITTY. I reckon I must have. [*His hair is all in ring-lets, and the stripes on his shirt now go around him in spirals.*] Thought I ought to come down and see what was happening in here.

SYMPATHY. You came to rescue us! Oh, you are kind. Could you undo my hands? [*He does so.*] We're stuck; the elevator won't work. And I found this book, but I can't get it open.

GRITTY. Caliban's book?

SYMPATHY. I suppose so. If we could find *him* and give him the book, maybe he'd unstick the eleva-tor for us.

FRED [*despondently*]. If he's got out, I don't suppose any-thing will ever fetch him back again.

SYMPATHY.   Surely he'd want to come back for his book?
             [*calling*] Caliban? Caliban? Oh, I'm fed up
             with those echoes. [*She begins to dance a
             dance of evocation, stretching up her arms
             to call* CALIBAN *down from wherever he has
             got to.*]
GRITTY.   I'll have a try on this thing. [*He sets up his
             little transmitter.*) Hello, hello, hello, Cali-
             ban, are you there, Caliban? We've found
             your book, we've found your book, Caliban.
             Over.
FRED [*singing*].
             O Caliban, where are you roaming?
             O can't you hear, the wires are humming?
             Where's our monster got to now?
             Trip no more your monstrous measure;
             Come back home, we've found your treasure,
             Thought we ought to let you know.
[*They all go on doing their thing for some time. At last
the light glows green.*]
SYMPATHY.   Look, look—
[*Elevator music; doors open. Green smoke.* CALIBAN *comes
out. He is also now recognizably* SAUL. *Doors shut.*]
SYMPATHY.   Father! [*more doubtfully*] Are you Father?
             Or are you Caliban?
CALIBAN.   Where is the book? Give me the book.
[CALIBAN *starts questing about; he looks so baleful that
they retreat from him nervously, and he becomes more and
more menacing.*]
GRITTY [*who has picked up book and is holding it behind
             him*]. Now look here, Caliban—we have

77

	every intention of giving you the book, but will you guarantee us safe conduct up to the lighthouse if we do?
CALIBAN.	No bargaining! [*He dives at* GRITTY *and manages to grab the book.*] Aha! Now! *Now* I have you all at my mercy. Now I shall go back into the world and wreak vengeance. I shall mow down the forests like mustard and cress. I shall trample the cities like carpets. I shall drink up the oceans like—like lemon squash. [*He swaggers about threateningly.*]
FRED.	Oh, no, you won't, chum. Don't be silly. You may have the book, but you still haven't got the key.
SYMPATHY.	Besides which, I don't believe you can read.
GRITTY.	So just pipe down and behave in a reasonable manner, will you?
MACAWMACK.	Stand on the right. Hold on to the rail. Dogs and pushchairs must be carried.

CALIBAN [*stares threateningly at them for another minute, then gives a long, lugubrious wail*]. Oh, it's true, it's true! I haven't got the key. It's lost. . . .

[*He completely caves in, sits down on a rock, hugging the book to his chest, wailing, and rocking backwards and forwards. Elevator music begins softly, then louder; the elevator doors open;* SYMPATHY, GRITTY, FRED, *and* MACAWMACK *file into the elevator; the doors close;* CALIBAN *continues to sit and wail. Lights gradually dim to darkness.* FRED *comes in again, spotlit; he pats* CALIBAN *awkwardly on the shoulder.*]

FRED.　　　　Do cheer up, old feller.

[*But* CALIBAN *continues to wail;* FRED *waits a moment, shrugs, then goes out.*]

SCENE SIX

The lighthouse. RUTH *knitting;* LORD BOSS *and* SUNUP *have skipping ropes and are seriously skipping and counting.*

BOSS.　　　　Thirty-seven,　　thirty-eight,　　thirty-nine, blast. . . . [*He trips over his rope and starts again.*] One, two, three. . . .

SUNUP.　　　Seventeen, eighteen. [*He skips much more slowly.* FEVER *comes in, also white.*]

FEVER.　　　What the blazes is going on? I feel all queer. Light-headed. Have we all got yellow fever— you two look very peculiar.

RUTH.　　　　Gracious, is that another of them?

SUNUP [*cheerfully*]. Hello, old Fever. Come to join the party? What happened to you? Where's Gritty?

FEVER.　　　I dunno. The last thing I remember is falling over the cliff. Am I delirious?

BOSS.　　　　Not delirious. Just dead.

RUTH.　　　　Fred *will* be pleased to have so many new friends. He never complained, but I know he felt it that Saul never took any notice of him.

[*Elevator music. Light glows green. Doors open.* SYMPATHY, GRITTY, *and* MACAWMACK *burst out. Doors shut.* FRED *ambles through the ordinary door.*]

SYMPATHY [*running to* RUTH, *hugging her*]. Are you all right, Mum?

RUTH.   Of course, I am, dearie. I've got all this company to keep me cheerful. Somebody kindly made me a cup of tea.

SYMPATHY [*looking around*]. Gosh!

FRED [*with satisfaction*]. We'll be able to play bridge on winter evenings.

BOSS [*peevish*]. That I should end up playing bridge in a lighthouse with the ghost of a straw-hat smuggler. What a come-down.

SYMPATHY.   But poor old Dad. Will he always stay down there in the cave with his miserable old grouch and his miserable old book?

RUTH.   Oh, I daresay he'll come up one day. And in the meantime I expect Fred will go down and keep him company sometimes. Won't you, Fred?

FRED.   Sure.

GRITTY.   Maybe somebody will find the key to the book some day.

FRED.   Dunno whether *that* would be such a good thing.

MACAWMACK. Place bag in locker, place coin in slot, turn key in lock.

RUTH.   Now, dearie, it's long past teatime. You'd

	better be on your way or you'll miss the last bus.
SYMPATHY.	Me? But aren't you coming, Mum? To see a doctor about your eyes?
RUTH.	No, dearie. It's too late for that. Being blind isn't so bad.
SYMPATHY.	Then I'll stay here and look after you.
RUTH.	That wouldn't do, lovey. You need to go back to town, where there's theaters for your dancing. I'll be all right. And you can always come home on a visit.
SYMPATHY [*distressed*].	But who'll look after you? And the lighthouse?
RUTH.	The young man will.
GRITTY [*simultaneously with* RUTH].	I will. It's just the sort of life that suits me. Plenty of time to sit in the sun and make up songs.
SYMPATHY.	But Mum—
GRITTY.	I'll keep an eye on her, Sympathy; don't you worry. You go and have your career; be a famous dancer.
SYMPATHY.	Don't *you* want a career?
GRITTY.	Not on your life!

[*He starts singing; they all join in.*]

I have other fish to fry,
Where the cow slips, there slip I,
In the lighthouse tower so high,
Snug as a mouse in an apple pie,
—Till the arrival of some other guy,
   Oh, how contentedly will we exist,

    Shining our light through the murk and
the mist,
    Shining our light through the murk and
the mist.

[*All the ghosts,* GRITTY *and* MACAWMACK *begin to dance.*
SYMPATHY *looks at them rather wistfully, longing to join
in, but* RUTH *kisses her good-bye so conclusively that she
goes out, though stopping for many backward looks.*]

      CURTAIN

SONGS

WORDS BY JOAN AIKEN
MUSIC BY JOHN SEBASTIAN BROWN

WHO IS CALIBAN?

This song is from pages 24 and 30

Who— is Ca - li - ban, who— is he?— Ev-
- ery - one seems— to won - der;— Sleep-
- ing down— be - low— the sea,— Snor-
- ing a - way like thun - der,— Fif-
- ty-five fath - oms— un - der.—

Eels he has where he oughta have hair;
Hands and feet are suckers;
Breathes in brine instead of air,
Makes a horrible ruckus,
Sounds like a boiler in bad repair.

Let's leave Caliban, let him lie;
It's tough enough to be him;
No use dragging him high and dry,
Nobody wants to see him.
Bye-bye, Caliban, bye-bye-bye.

FULL FATHOM FIVE

This song is from page 26

Full fath-om five thy bro-ther— lies, His

but-tons— turned to— had-docks' eyes,—

No - thing of him now is— found Save— a

ghost that— floats a - round Two feet— off—

— the— ground, Some might find this ra-ther

strange, But not old— Fred; he likes the— change.

WHO DOTH NOT WANT A THING

This song is from page 31

Who doth not want a thing Ex - cept a

place to sing And a fire to warm his

feet In win - ter's wet and sleet,

Give o - ver,— give o - ver,— give o - ver,—

The book of all know - ledge, As good as a col-

- lege, Some know - how— is bet-ter

than fruit - less en - dea - - vour.—

MOONCUSSERS' SONG

This song is from pages 39 and 72

When Force Twelve Gale doth loud-ly— blow,— And whirl-pools whirl and glow-worms glow,— And birds sit— brood - ing— in the— snow,— And Gulf Stream re - vers-eth to - wards— Mex - i - co, And Mo-ther Car-ey's chicks are— hatched, And main -. sail— do split and— got-ta be patched, Hey ding - a - ling We— sing,— For all e - vents— but ours are— scratched.

When nights are black with mist and murk,
That's when the Mooncussers get to work,
With pick and pike and spike and dirk
Behind each rock a bloke doth lurk,
And keels are split and hulls are stove
And wrecks cast up in every cove.
   Why then we sing
   Hey ding-a-ding
For this is the weather we approve.

PATIENCE

This song is from page 44

COME UNTO THIS ROCKBOUND COAST

This song is from page 53

Come un - to this rock-bound coast, Ev-'ry ghost; A-ny spook who turns up here Gets a beer; Wel-come, wel-come to our shore, There's al-ways room for just one more, Hark, hark, Peek-a-boo The owls do bark, To-wit-to-woo, Hark, hark, I hear Dol-phins sing-ing far and near, A. E. I. O. U.

Repeat last three bars several times.

91

KATE

This song is from page 58

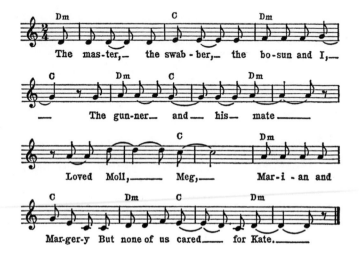

The mas-ter,— the swab-ber,— the bo-sun and I,—

— The gun-ner— and— his— mate—

Loved Moll,— Meg,— Mar-i-an and

Mar-ger-y But none of us cared— for Kate.—

O CALIBAN

This song is from page 77

O Cal-i - ban, where are___ you roam - ing?___

O can't you hear, the___ wires___ are hum - ming

Where's our mon-ster___ got___ to___ now?___

Trip no more___ your mon - strous mea - sure,

Come back home,___ we've found___ your trea - sure,

Thought we ought to___ let___ you___ know.___

LIGHTHOUSE SONG

This song is from page 81

THE PLAY was produced by the Unicorn Theatre for Young People and directed by Ursula Jones for the Puffin Players. It was first performed on April 7th, 1973, at the Young Vic, London, England.

CHARACTERS IN ORDER OF APPEARANCE

SAUL BILKANCHOR lighthouse keeper of Sabertooth Lighthouse	Siôn Probert
RUTH his wife	Matyelok Gibbs
FRED Saul's brother	Gary Fairhall
SYMPATHY Saul's daughter	Jacqueline Andrews
LORD BOSS	Eric Leroy
FEVER	Richard Jason
GRITTY	Ian Ruskin
SUNUP	Terry O'Sullivan
MACAWMACK	Marina McConnell
WAITRESS	Marina McConnell

About the Author

JOAN AIKEN, well known in a dozen countries for her mystery-thrillers, has published nearly a score of books for adults and juveniles alike.

Daughter of poet Conrad Aiken and sister of two professional writers, she was born in England and began writing at the age of five, because, as she says, "Writing is just the family trade."

Her varied career includes work with the United Nations in London, a stint in advertising, and a number of stories published in such magazines as *Vogue* and *Ellery Queen's Mystery Magazine*. The author of such modern classics as *The Wolves of Willoughby Chase,* Miss Aiken has won the prestigious Manchester Guardian Award for Children's Literature. And her novel *The Whispering Mountain* was chosen runner-up for the Carnegie Medal for children's books.

Joan Aiken wrote her first play, *Winterthing*, when both her son and daughter became engaged in educational theater workshop activities. Her interest in children's theater continues with the publication of *The Mooncusser's Daughter*. She lives in Sussex, England, where, in addition to writing, she paints, gardens, and collects nineteenth-century children's literature.